Grandma's Secret Letter

written by Maggie S. Davis
illustrated by John Wallner

HOLIDAY HOUSE, NEW YORK

Printed in the United States of America
First Edition

Library of Congress Cataloging in Publication Data

Davis, Maggie S 1942–
Grandma's secret letter.

SUMMARY: A child's secret letter from Grandma explains all the directions for getting to her house, including all the elves, ghosts, witches, and dragons she is to deliver messages to along the way.
[1. Fantasy] I. Wallner, John C. II. Title.
PZ7.D2952Gr [E] 80-23331
ISBN 0-8234-0382-3 AACR1

For Jenny and Joel
M.S.D.

For Mona
J.W.

This morning
I nearly flew out of bed.
Grandma was waiting for me in her house
on a hilltop far away.
In the desk near my window
was her secret letter.

"Cook breakfast
for the tiny elf who's waiting
in the garden. Don't forget to say
I'll see him soon."
That's what Grandma wrote at the beginning.

So I served the elf some porridge
in a yellow buttercup and asked him
riddles while he ate.
Then he led me to the road
that said TO GRANDMA'S.

"When you come to the place
where the tall trees rise,"
Grandma said in her secret letter,
"blow a kiss to the ghost that splashes
in the stream. Poor thing! She's lonesome for me."

I blew a kiss—more than one—and was given
a ride to the opposite shore.
There, the ghost and I danced brightly
to the tune a rabbit played
on his viola.

Around the bend, a crystal mountain
blocked my way. It was high
and far too slippery to cross.

"Put your arms around the weeping bear
that sits in the road," Grandma's
letter said. "He misses my hugs."

I squeezed the bear hard
and helped him wipe away his tears.
Then he flashed a cheery smile
and threw me in the air—once, twice—

then over the mountain gently
to the spot where the grass witch
caught me warmly in her arms.

"Listen to the stories the grass witch tells,"
Grandma told me in her letter.
"Except for me she has hardly any company."

I listened well
and wove ribbons through
the grass witch's hair.

Between her braids she made
a space where I could sleep.

Loud buzzing sounds
awakened me soon after.
The grass witch was gone.
There in the deep of a tiny tangled tree
slept twin snoring cats.
"Sing to them sweetly.

No one's good to them but me,"
Grandma scribbled in her letter.
So I sang them a lullaby.
I fanned them while they snored.
And later on they joined their tails
so I could swing.

Next, I headed through
the darkest part of the thick woods
where the road twisted five terrible times.
Where the wild wizard lived.
Where the wicked white dragons
roared from where they hid.

"They're more wonderful than bad,"
Grandma's letter said.
"Just show them that you care as much as I do."

I prepared an elegant tea and
invited each guest personally.
The wizard brought cakes filled
with sweet jam.
The dragons, armfuls
of fluttering butterflies.

After tea, we discussed the shapes
of clouds and distant moons.

"Let me know when you're close to my door."
That's how Grandma signed her letter.
So I whooped down the road
and shouted—"Grandma!"—up the hill.
I knew she'd be at home and glad to see me.

Well, she was—
and quite pleased
to find more company.